ZERO HOUR ON THE GRID

ART DICKERSON

ISBN: 978-1-4907-7257-8 (sc)
ISBN: 978-1-4907-7259-2 (hc)
ISBN: 978-1-4907-7258-5 (e)

Library of Congress Control Number: 2016906098

Trafford rev. 04/16/2016

 www.trafford.com

North America & international
toll-free: 1 888 232 4444 (USA & Canada)
fax: 812 355 4082

ZERO HOUR FOR THE GRID

The car pulled up to the gate of the San Francisco consulate. The guard, recognizing it as attached to the operation, opened the gate and saluted. He then smiled at the driver. The man on the back seat he recognized as the chief of station, in charge of domestic intelligence operations. He did not recognize the second passenger, but her face and clothes said she was from the motherland. He watched the car drive through and then closed the gate. All seemed well at the consulate.

"I was told that your consulate was nicely kept, but I see that was an understatement. It is beautiful and securely private."

"Thank you, we value privacy greatly and who can argue with beauty? Let's step inside I am eager to hear what you bring from the motherland. I know that you are scheduled to deliver a technical paper *Analysis of Macroeconomics Using Modern Control Theory*. It sounds very technical, even for the director of the the economics bureau."

"Let's talk about it when we are inside."

Inside the consulate they sat in a room shielded electromagnetically and sonically and sipped slowly at their cups of Earl Grey tea. "The paper is not my primary mission. Are you are aware of the nature of the U.S. electric power grid?"

"I know that it delivers the energy to operate nearly everything in the U.S. Including the lights in this room, the stove that brewed this tea and even the pump that put gas into the car that brought us from the airport."

"Let's suppose for a moment that it was shut down."

"It would be a catastrophe unless it could be brought back up quickly."

"Suppose it took three days to bring it back."

"That would be terrible, we would be without lights, heat, even food."

"Suppose it took three weeks."

"My god, hospitals shut down, no police, no food, no communication. Total catastrophe!"

"We are going to take down the grid. That's the purpose of my visit to San Francisco. We need your help in setting the correct action and the timing for maximum effect. Are you with me and your government, or do we have a problem?"

There was a silence in the room. The Chief of Station's jaw hung wide open for several seconds. With a jerk it closed. "You mean that the motherland has decided to punish America by taking down the grid ?"

"That is correct, but you have not answered my question. Are you ready to play your role in this endeavor, or must you be removed back to the motherland?"

More seconds passed. "I am an official of the motherland. I will play my role, but I must ask questions and voice opinions in secret. If my name ever got out, I could be killed."

"Do not worry about your name. You and a few other Chiefs of Station will be referred to by names that designate your location. For example, you will always be Francis in any conversation or communication on this matter. If we have an associate in Philadelphia, he will be Phil. This is absolutely essential for security purposes. The NSA and FBI, as you know, are reading all consulate communications. Thus, any reference to our associates will be in American names. My name will be Randy, because I move about. Also, the triggering event will be named 'Eddy'. Thus a text message to Phil might read, 'Eddy is arriving on American Airlines about 1 pm Monday. Please be sure to pick him up.'"

"I see, Randy. The message would not look suspicious to either humans or digital 'crawlers' which scour messages. Very simple, very clever. However, we must be careful to communicate only when necessary. The heavier traffic might in itself raise suspicions."

"Very good. Now we will need to talk with a student in Los Angeles. He is already part of the plan. Selected by the chief himself and for this task named Cal. He knows about the plan for the grid. Cal is from the motherland and here on a green card studying electrical engineering for his doctorate. He has a contract to study the vulnerability of the grid. We can drive down after I have delivered my paper. The paper is not a fake, but a good technical analysis and excellent excuse for my traveling."

TECHNOLOGY CONSULTATION

The room in the Los Angeles consulate was a mirror image of that in San Francisco. Randy introduced the third person in the room. "This is Cal, he is a doctoral student at USC on a green card. His thesis is on the vulnerability of the U. S. power grid to total failure. Cal, this is Francis, Station Chief in San Francisco. You can speak openly with him."

"It's an honor to meet you Francis. And especially to meet you Randy, I've learned of your upcoming paper on Macroeconomics. It sounds very interesting."

"It's good to meet you Cal, I compliment you on your thesis work. Tell me, is there tight secrecy around your topic?"

"None. The technologists are aware of the vulnerability. The government is deeply concerned about the effects, but knows of no solution. They are funding some study in hopes of finding a possible solution. That's not in sight now."

Randy looked directly at Cal. "Suppose you tell us how the grid might come down?"

"Well, there are four ways. First, a bombardment from a large sun spot. When such an explosion occurs on the suns' surface, there is a huge burp of charged particles called a coronal mass ejection or CME. It shoots out away from the sun for a brief period. Usually this just goes off into space with no effect on the earth. However, if the hole in the suns' atmosphere is aligned with the earth, this huge stream of CME enters through the earth's atmosphere and induces high electric currents in the grid. This may burn out key pieces of equipment. That happened in 1989 in Canada and took down the Canadian grid."

"How long did it take to get back up?"

"In the Canadian case they had a good stock of spare parts and were up in a few days. However, if large transformers are involved, it can be weeks or months. Those things are huge and very expensive. Spares are rare. Should I explain the sun spots in detail?"

"That's not necessary, although my doctorate was in economics, I've studied physics. I'm with you."

"Well, a second means to take the grid down is by human attack. This was demonstrated in California recently when a substation was shut down by rifle fire that punctured the cooling equipment for the transformers. That was well planned as the rifle cartridges showed no finger prints. It almost took off a portion of the grid in California. A recent study of the U.S. Grid has shown that a simultaneous loss of just nine select stations out of 55,000 could bring down the whole grid."

"How many people do you think were involved in that rifle attack"

"No one is sure, but my guess would be four or five. It was quick and very well planned."

"So to take down nine or ten stations simultaneously by gunfire would require around fifty people."

"Yes and considerable communication between them beforehand. That might be a weakness and it could attract the NSA and CIA."

Cal stopped momentarily and then said, "A third means is by cyber attack, getting into the computer control of key stations and taking them down. It isn't clear how long it might take to recover from this. Studying that is part of my thesis. However, there are a little over 2000 stations that can be communicated with via the internet."

"But we need not attack all 2000 at once, maybe only 10 or 12?"

"That would do it. A fourth means is much less recognized. This is by electro-magnetic pulse or EMP. When a nuclear weapon is detonated there is a brief but intense release of gamma radiation known as 'prompt gamma'."

"Would it be possible to cover the entire U.S. with one detonation?"

"Yes, if a reasonable sized weapon were discharged 300 miles outside the atmosphere, the territory directly below, about the size of the U.S., would be radiated enough to destroy the electronic controls of the power stations."

"Would that have to be an ICBM?"

"No, the weapon might be on board an ordinary satellite unnoticed for years."

"Wait a minute, Cal Is this just theory?"

"No. In a test shot in the Pacific, a weapon was detonated outside the atmosphere and electric stations were damaged in Hawaii over 1000 miles away. Actually green 'northern lights' were seen over Hawaii."

"So the vulnerability of the grid isn't theory, it's happened. The question is one of severity and how long it takes to restore the grid?"

"Randy, I could'nt put it better."

Unknown to Cal and Francis, all of this had been logged on a small black recorder sown into the center of Randy's generous black bra. She leaned back and with a slight touch to the middle of her blouse turned off the recorder.

"Thank you very much, Cal, you have been extremely helpful to the motherland. That will not be forgotten."

WHEN AND HOW DO WE ACT?

Randy had delivered her paper at the east coast conference and was back in the San Francisco consulate. She and Francis sat in chairs on a section of lawn bounded by small trees and bushes. They paused briefly and she said, "Is it safe to talk here?

"Almost as safe as the 'quiet room'. There are white noise generators in the bushes that obscure any sound that would reach a microphone or recorder. You might hear a slight rustling sound like bugs moving in dry leaves. And, we are visually obscured by the trees so that no one can read our lips. I think we can talk safely."

"I'd like to hear your ideas on when and how we start to take down the grid. We don't want to kill a lot of people, although some deaths will be inevitable. The prime objective is to ruin America's financial reputation worldwide. It must be the end of the American dollar as the world's reserve currency. If there were major casualties and the cause was ever traced to the motherland, there would be great trouble. Death for you and me would be inescapable."

"Well Randy, to reduce casualties the event should occur in mid-summer and avoid effects of lost residential heating. Also, at that time there will be food crops maturing. However, transporting them to cities would be a problem. So, I'd say between mid-June and October a span of 4 1/2 months."

"Would there be any advantage of beginning in the first year after an election so that a new set of politicians would be in charge at the federal level?"

"True that bonding and trust would not yet have been established. However, those qualities have been notably lacking in recent decades. Remember that after the event there would be almost no communication available with the internet, commercial radio and cell phones out of order. Only hard-wired phones and CB radio would be available along with some ham radio on batteries. In short, command and control would be greatly limited."

Randy thought for a moment. "OK, lets say that mid-June to October will be the time. What's your view on method?"

"We may want to talk further with Cal, but I have some tentative views. For example, the use of human attack seems risky. That would require a lot of communication and money beforehand. It would be hard to avoid the notice and decoding by NSA and the FBI. Then the communication at the zero hour would be a further problem. I would put human attack at the bottom of the list."

"I agree with you, Francis. There is also the problem of information leakage from fifty people who would want others to know how powerful they can be. Let's put it off the table for the time being. What about cyber attack?"

"That seems to be a good approach. However, we should talk again with Cal to learn what protection moves are underway. One very positive thing is that it might require no more than five or six people each using two computers to do the hacking. Coordination among these five or six should be easy and would not attract attention."

"Would it be possible to have the original internet addresses for these hackers to be in the U.S.?"

"Yes, also they could use Facebook and Twitter daily so as not to attract attention. In fact they might be able to use their Facebook pages to coordinate the attack time using some simple code such as *I'm going to a movie tonight with Paul at 7:00 pm we'll have a late dinner afterward*. Looks innocent unless you know that Paul doesn't exist."

Randy smiled. "I love it! And with only five or six people this should be secret and manageable!"

Francis bent his head down then said. "One thing I've been pondering is the sunspot attack. It has much to commend it as the source is not on the earth. However, we have no control over it. But there is a possibility. Cal said that typically there is a period of half a day to a day after the explosion on the sun is visible and the time that the CME strikes the earth. Suppose we could coordinate a cyber attack to occur just after the opening moments of a sunspot strike. It would then appear that the stations lost by cyber means were just a follow on to the sunspot. Later analysis might show a difference, but communication at the time would be so bad that immediate analysis would be impossible."

"Most interesting Francis, but how do you coordinate the cyber attack in the middle of a sunspot CME?"

"That's going to take some thought and planning, but we can discuss it with Cal. Looks like we need a second meeting with him."

"OK Francis, how do you see the EMP attack?

"It would be so big and unusual that there will be a much longer recovery time. Something that bothers me is that Northern Radiation and Air Defense, or NORAD will track the satellite after it leaves synchronous orbit. They may not know or guess what is about to happen, but they will know who put the satellite up there. NORAD has just moved back into It's original radiation-proof home inside Cheyenne mountain in the Rockies. They will be able to analyze the satellite data immediately and know who caused the attack."

"So you see the EMP is a last ditch stand if all else fails?"

"You would know better than I whether the motherland wishes to go that far."

"Alright Francis, let's talk about a meeting with Cal before we go inside. I think it might be well for him to go to the Los Angeles consulate so that there is no question occurring to NSA as to why he goes all the way to San Francisco for any minor item that could be taken care of in Los Angeles."

"That's wise. Let me know when you can go and I'll ask Los Angeles to have him come in on something small, say a review of the mother country address for his Green Card."

As Randy rose from her chair to go inside the consulate, she touched the center of her blouse, turning off the recorder.

* * *

Cal was to report about his green card. He was shown directly into the quiet room and knew when he saw the other occupants it he was not there for a review of the card. They shook hands all around and Francis started the conversation.

"Cal, we need additional information about the grid, specifically what efforts are underway to arm it against a crash and how long it might take to recover from one. We have decided that the attack will be in late summer, say around mid August. We've ruled out human attack and the EMP method. So what is underway to strengthen the grid against cyber attack or CME?"

"I think you've made good decisions on the method. There are some moves underway to stiffen grids against collapse. For example, in China there is the start of High Voltage DC or HVDC ties that can bring a remote energy source to an urban load from any distance. HVDC is also popular in Europe and Brasil. In America things move slowly. There is talk of a 'Tres Amigas' DC station at Clovis, New Mexico to permit high energy exchange among the three parts of the U.S. Grid, the Eastern Grid, Western Grid and Texas Grid. This would be a great help in preventing collapse. But at present there are just a few such links in the U.S."

"When will that 'Tres Amigas' station start operation."

"Not for sometime, maybe three or four years. They have just now obtained an OK to buy a reserve on the necessary land."

Randy smiled. "Ah, great! Let's assume that we are talking about a zero hour in the next two years."

"Then I think you will see little change in the U.S. grid, maybe some in Canada, but not here. The grid is owned by so many different companies that getting agreement on action and money is nearly impossible."

"Tell us a little about the vulnerability of the present grid."

"In general, concentrations of large load without large local generation are instable when the load peaks. That's why your August timing is good. The air conditioning load will peak in mid afternoon and the city areas will be only marginally stable. There is one large, remote HVDC link on the west coast from the Columbia river dam and generators at Dalles, Oregon to Los Angeles, CA. This might stabilize part of Los Angeles if other nearby loads are abandoned.

However, that is a rarity, but it illustrates how different situations occur locally."

Randy pursed her lips. "Maybe we should discuss the situation of communication in the face of a grid collapse. What will be available and for how long. Much will depend on communication to put the grid back together won't it?"

"You just made a good point. It is related to what method is bringing the grid down. For example, if this is from a large CME from the sun, you will probably lose many satellites with a consequent failure of most internet and many phone routes for a long period of time. There are only about one half of U.S. phones on direct hard-wired connection. You remember them with the old rotary dials. They connect directly to the lines that operate from batteries at the phone companies exchange. True, they are recharged from the grid so they will eventually fail after the batteries are discharged and the fuel for emergency generators is used up. But, that will take a few days. So You'll have hard-wired phones for that period. Communication with Asia and Europe is by submarine cable which has its own electric supply at well guarded underground installations, good for about 30 days."

"So what about the results of cyber attack?"

"Pretty much the same except that satellites will be available. Local power sources could be cobbled together on the ground for communication to other similar sites."

"How long would it take to get the grid back together after a cyber attack?"

"There's no single answer as it gets into the amount of equipment damage that occurs during the collapse. However, I think you should expect that some local parts of the grid, where load and generation were well matched, might be back in a day or two. A few parts might not be back for a week or so."

"And if the cyber attack is coordinated with a solar event, how long then?"

"Really impossible to say as the variables are so great. But some places would not be back up for weeks. The whole scheme, including satellites, not for many months."

"Again, Cal, thank you for your great help. Now I think the consulate really does want to review your green card. They told me that you had applied for citizenship when you first came over and that you are close to being in the quota. Congratulations."

Francis and Randy had lunch at the consulate and then were driven back to San Francisco.

SETTING THE PLAN IN MOTION

Francis and Randy were back at the San Francisco consulate enjoying a drink in the outdoor garden. The white noise generators attracted a bird which assumed the noise was bugs in the leaves on the ground. The bird lit and finding no bugs, took off immediately for more productive areas.

"Randy, I'm honored that the motherland selected me to work with you on this project. However, I'm puzzled about the choice. There are many excellent chiefs of station at the consulates and the embassy in America. Why am I honored?"

"The motherland government has great respect for your intelligence and your loyalty, but as you say there are others. Your physical location in San Francisco was a factor. You see, we need someone to coordinate the action down to the last minute. If we in any way use the solar flare, the damage will be at higher latitudes and move from East to West at about 650 miles per hour. For example, Boston would be hit first and Seattle hit last about four hours later. So you would be the 'last man standing' and be in the best spot to do the coordination. Also, San Francisco has excellent airline connections and a good land line connection to the trans-pacific cable."

"So the motherland has been thinking about this for some time?"

"You can assume that. Now lets talk about how we put this team together. We will need the cooperation of another five or six chiefs of station across the country to do the actual cyber attack. I have Cal's list of electric stations that need to be put down. The men we select should be close to these locations. One is about 100 miles east of you here. So that falls naturally to you. Another is in Texas, close to Houston. What do you know of our man there?"

"He is unquestionably loyal, but not the brightest penny in the box. Could we count on another one nearby to lead him?"

"I don't like it. One layer of personnel is enough. We'll just do without Houston. We also need a man in Pittsburg, PA and others in Chicago and St. Louis."

"Pittsburg will work out well, he's loyal, brilliant and works well alone. However, I worry a little about Chicago, he is not very bright and too sensitive about it. He does not take instruction well. Could St. Louis be the alternative?"

"No, we need St. Louis in addition to Chicago. Suppose we get the Chicago man replaced by another from elsewhere in the U.S. Who do you think might do the job well?"

"The man in Boston is very loyal and brilliant, he's skilled in computer programming too. Do you think that would work?"

"It would work beautifully."

"Alright, we will go with Dallas, Pittsburg and St. Louis plus a new man in Chicago and myself here in San Francisco. I'm glad we do not have to involve the embassy in Washington or the consulate in New York. I've never fully understood their viewpoints."

"I agree with you Francis. With the leakage of information in Washington, D.C., we couldn't trust the embassy. I have a special job for New York. Let's talk about our man there, you had problems with his viewpoint?"

"He's much too close to the criminal element in New York. He's smart alright, but a little on the lazy side. He thinks too much about money."

"That may work out well! What we need is one human attack that is essential. We need a bomb to explode in the distribution station in Manhattan on 12th street. It supplies the entire southern end of Manhattan including the financial district and the stock exchanges.

Taking it out of service for a long period will be a key step to ruining America's financial reputation worldwide."

"Let me talk with him, he will probably want to go along as he hates the rich Americans. I will get back to you with his response."

INTEGRATING THE TEAM AND PLAN

Randy continued her American trip to the four additional locations and discussed the plan with each of the station chiefs. She bound each to her personally when she removed the black bra. None of them noticed the recorder when the matching black panties slipped to the floor. Later, each was sworn to silence, thinking that he was the sole receiver of this elite treatment. A pleased but tired Randy took a flight back to the motherland.

A week later the station chief in Chicago was called back to the motherland for a new assignment. He was replaced by the man from Boston. The new Chico demonstrated his computer programming skills when he invented a game based on an actual hack into a major grid station. It allowed wandering through the control options of the station. He also disguised it as a pure game, then made a CD which was mailed to the other hackers as a training aide. When summer came all of the hackers could wander through the controls of their target stations as easily as they walked through their own abodes.

Francis talk with York in Manhattan took place in the quiet room at the consulate. The first response was definite interest in putting a knife to the rich "one percent" and next was how could he personally make some money on the deal. Francis had him right. After two days for him to sound out the possibilities they met again in the quiet room.

"Alright, Francis I've found the man for you. Name is Ivan, works for Con Edison and cleans up the 12th street station once a week. He agrees to put a large bomb in the closet where cleaning supplies are kept. He will trigger it by cell phone from his apartment which is in the next block. He's tested the phone and it can be picked up inside the station. Problem is, he wants a wad of money to pull this off. Points out he may lose his job if there's no place to clean up."

"How much does he want?"

"He says $25,000. will cover it. Maybe I can knock him down a little, but not much."

"Tell you what, York. Here's $50,000. You bargain with him. Also make sure it is absolutely secret after it happens if you know what I mean. Then whatever is left over is yours. But I mean really secret. And if it doesn't come off on the assigned time you'd do well to leave town permanently." York smiled.

"You'll receive instructions on timing by internet. It will advise you of a visitor from the motherland named Eddy and instruct you to meet him at the airport on a specific date and time. After that it's up to you."

"I'm with you Francis, It will be as you say."

Francis took a heavy envelope out of his briefcase and handed it to York. His facial grimace validated the threat about leaving town permanently.

The first year passed quietly with no CME. The team practiced regularly with encouragement from Randy who traveled to various universities to talk on her technical paper, stopping in route at the consulates. All appeared normal. Then a CME occurred.

WHAT NORAD AND THE WHITEHOUSE KNEW

General North, sat at his desk inside the Cheyenne mountain home of NORAD. He was CINCNORAD or commander in chief. He was worried about the pictures from the Solar Dynamics Observatory, SDO. These showed a large solar eruption a day earlier. It looked like The start of a CME. This might mean trouble for the military's satellites. The phone rang.

"General North."

"General, this is Colonel Luke in surveillance. We just had a satellite pass over Iceland. It measured a proton flux level about twice that of the 1989 solar flare. We have been aware of a large sun spot for 24 hours, but this is the first indication that we have of a CME and it's a big one. It might be wise to advise the White House that POTUS should not go aboard a plane or helicopter. In fact, this is large enough that it might suggest movement to the underground Command Center, the UCC."

"You are sure of this reading?"

"Yes Sir. This satellite is well shielded and all other readings remain normal."

"How soon will the CME reach the eastern edge of the U.S.?"

"A little over 2 hours."

"Can you advance that satellite's orbit so that each time it crosses north latitude 75 degrees it's following the CME?"

"Yes sir.'

"Do It and stay on this line."

On a second line the general called White House security."

"Security, major Brown."

"Brown, this is General North, CINCNORAD. I have an urgent message for the security commander."

"Sir, at this hour I am the senior officer present."

"Alright. We have a very large solar event on the way to the U.S. We expect it will be much larger than the event that took out the Canadian electric grid in Quebec. There will be danger to aircraft. We suggest that POTUS not board any aircraft or helicopter. As the storm develops, we may advise that POTUS move to the Underground Command Center, UCC. Do you understand?"

"Yes Sir. POTUS is not to be airborne. I will start the action here. There may be a later move to the UCC."

"Good. Keep this line open or transfer me to another line that will be the control of security."

The general turned from the phone to push a button on his communication panel. An aide immediately appeared.

"Get the Canadian general here and let me have two additional aides in this room."

"Yes sir."

The Canadian general, second in command at NORAD, entered and with a smile asked,

"What's up. Things seem a little busy out there."

"I have bad news for us both, but particularly for you. Do you recall the solar incident that took the Canadian grid down?"

"I'm Canadian, how could I forget it?"

"We have another similar event on the way. It will arrive in a little less than 2 hours in your eastern provinces. We have this from a satellite that was passing over Iceland and measured a proton flux density about twice that of the earlier incident. I expect you will want to communicate with home base?"

"You are sure of this?"

"I've already called the White House.

"Thank you. I'm on my way."

Ninety minutes later a new report came in as the same satellite again crossed the path of the CME. The aide holding the phone from surveillance motioned to the general and held out the phone.

"General North."

"Sir we have a second reading from the satellite. It is essentially the same as the first and the readings in the equator area were zero, so we believe it. We estimate the CME will strike the state of Maine in about thirty minutes and Boston shortly after. It will be over Washington in about 50 minutes."

"Thank you. Please keep this line open and maintain the satellite on its tracking orbit."

"Aide, tell the Canadian general we have a second confirmation of the CME."

General North picked up the phone to the White House and asked who was on the line.

"General White, aide to the president. I am now in charge of security."

"White, we have a second satellite confirmation of the CME. I suggest now that you move POTUS to the UCC. The proton flux will be on your location in less than 50 minutes."

"Agreed. We will start the action immediately. There may be a delay getting the senior congressional people in place, but we will move POTUS now."

An hour later the general received a call from the UCC. The voice announced itself as Gates, the president's chief of staff.

"You'll be glad to know that the president is now here underground as are the senior members of Congress and your associates from the Pentagon. The president's chef has examined the kitchen and the food stores. He says that we are in good shape for 30 days. I'm pleased at that as good meals make for good policy. Of course we won't need it, but it's good to know that it's there"

"I'm glad you will be well cared for, sir. However, we have some immediate news from Canada. The proton stream has struck eastern Newfoundland and there is serious damage to the electric supply there. I fear we will have severe damage here, beginning in under an hour. Do you have the head of the Federal Energy Reliability Commission, FERC, there in your location?"

"No, we had not thought he would be necessary to the management of the Government!"

"You may wish to reconsider that. The people in FERC have been concerned with failure of the grid for several years. His experience and thinking may be helpful during the restoration."

"You mean you think we may really lose the electric grid?"

"Mr. Gates, no one can predict with certainty, but I think it is likely enough that we must plan on it happening. Are you on emergency power now?"

"Not yet, but we ---"

At that moment there was a sputtering and loud frying noise on the phone. It was safe, but the equipment at each end depended on the grid or emergency generators for power. After two minutes the voice came back.

"All right general. There may be something to what you say. We have lights back on now and all seems to be in order."

"Can you reach New York on your red phone?"

"One moment. No, it doesn't seem to answer and there is a lot of noise on the line. I'll get back to you."

General North drew a deep sigh as he prayed for a world free of politicians.

* * *

The U.S. was not the only power with satellites observing the approaching CME. The motherland satellite provided essentially the same data to it's monitoring base. The arrival of Eddy was phoned from motherland to Francis and on to York. Francis in turn announced the arrival of various passengers to Pitt, Chico, Louie and Dale at the appropriate times.

MONDAY AUGUST 15, NOON
EASTERN STANDARD TIME

"Eddy will arrive at 1:00 pm on August 15. I hope you can meet him on American Airlines at the airport."

The message went by cell phone to York. At 12:55 the CME hit New York. At 1:00 pm an explosion occurred at the Con Ed 12th street station in Manhattan. Thick black smoke blew violently from the vents. The lights of lower Manhattan went out. The New York Stock Exchange went on diesel backup. When it was learned that all lower Manhattan had lost power, the decision was made to freeze the market value at the time of power loss and wait for the brokerage offices return to operation. That would not happen for quite a time. The diesel backup was later shut down to maintain 8 hours of fuel supply. The U.S. financial market was dead.

The proton flux of the CME killed many satellites with inadequate shielding. People immediately noticed the failure of cell phone links and several internet communication paths. Portions of the electric grid failed in Boston, Albany and Long Island when the proton stream increased current in the conductors. These shutdowns spread westward slowly as generating stations were presented with more load than they could supply.

22

Pitt was the next to act. He hacked into two major stations in western Pennsylvania and eastern Ohio. He simply took them off line. The failure of the grid accelerated as more stations found it impossible to supply the load that was required of them. That included several nuclear generating plants. When they left the grid, the emergency diesel generators switched on to power just the station controls. These continued to run until the fuel supply reached the point of only eight hours remaining. Then they switched off to retain the ability to come on line later. That would turn out to be much later. With the loss of the nuclear plants, the complete grid west of Manhattan began to segment.

Chico hacked into two major stations one to the east and one to the southwest of Chicago. As with Pittsburg, this accelerated disconnect of generating stations and inbound transmission lines from the grid. That in turn took several nuclear plants off line, using their diesel emergency supplies just for controls.

Louie in St. Louis did the same hacking job on two stations to the east. The result was similar. By now the eastern grid was off except for a few local supplies, such as the hydro generation in the TVA district.

Dale in Dallas took out, by hacking, one station to the east and one to the south. This totally isolated the Texas grid from both the east and west grids. It initiated failures southward all the way to Houston.

Francis watched all of this in San Francisco using first cable TV and when that failed, his satellite dish which presented a TV image soon torn into shreds with intermediate loss of sound. He saw that the grid failure was proceeding much as Randy and he had planned. He went on line with his hard-wired AT&T internet line and hacked into two stations, one the main north-south California link and the other a link to San Francisco from the north. Shortly his lights went out and the TV failed. He picked up his old hard-wired AT&T phone and found that it still had a dial tone. The Diablo canyon nuclear plant on the central coast had been intentionally spared and when he dialed a number in the motherland the call went through via the Trans-Pacific Cable whose U.S. link was only a few miles from Diablo Canyon. He wished his "grandfather" a happy birthday and reported that the recent book which was a gift from him was very interesting and historically accurate. "Grandfather" was greatly pleased and called his daughter Randy to share the news.

PRIVATE LIVES

Chicago, Il. 1:30 pm: Sue and Jerry lived in the suburbs where she worked as the secretary to the manger of the local Walmart. Jerry was the assistant manager at the local Home Depot store. Sue's boss called her into the office and closed the door.

"I don't know what is up, but I've had a call from the head shed saying to prepare for an unplanned shutdown with loss of the ATM and charge card ability. Would you please take my credit card and get $100. cash from the ATM and buy rice, water bottles and a propane cylinder for my grill? If you wish to use your credit card for your own purchases, you are welcome, but hurry."

Sue ran out, grabbed a shopping cart and headed for the ATM and $100. for him and $40. for herself. Then to the clerks where she duplicated his purchases for herself. The charge cards worked, but on the way back the store lights dipped then went to emergency battery. She saw people cursing the ATM and clerks shouting "cash only". Whatever was up it was large. The boss thanked her and sorted the purchases into two carts.

"If the lights are still out in an hour, we will shut down and you can go home." They were. She did. On the way it seemed a good idea to fill the car's gas tank. At the station there was a long waiting line and a hand-lettered sign reading, "unable to pump".

Arriving home she saw Jerry's station wagon in the driveway. He was in the living room with a cardboard box of purchases. "The boss knew something from headquarters. He said I should buy extra batteries for our flashlights and a pair of Citizen's Band, CB radio handsets with extra batteries for them too. He says we can communicate through the CB units. The lights went out, so we shut down. We could only sell for cash and you'd be surprised how little cash is in folks pockets today."

Sue showed her purchases. Jerry said a Scotch on the rocks would go well after this weird day. He poured the scotch and started toward the kitchen for ice cubes. On the way he stopped at the bathroom. After using the toilet, he noticed the tank did not seem to refill. At the sink to wash his hands, all he got was a short stream and then a burp of droplets.

"Sue, we're gonna need those water bottles sooner than we thought. Maybe you could get the ice cubes? I think a scotch on the rocks is a very good idea."

Calgary, Alberta, Canada 7:00 pm - Marie and Jacques moved from Quebec to a ranch they bought outside Calgary. The decision had been as good as they expected. Their herd of cattle, though not huge was large enough to make money. Their truck garden was in the full production of late summer. Their chickens produced a steady supply of eggs and an occasional fryer. They sat on the porch, watching the setting sun. Marie looked worried, saying: "The electricity has been off for hours now, perhaps we should light one of the kerosene lanterns from the barn and start thinking of dinner."

Jacques went to the barn and returned with a glowing lamp. Marie had begun to survey the refrigerator and mentally put together a dinner based on what would spoil first if the lights stayed off. They had lived through the grid failure in Quebec and some ideas just came naturally.

"Jacques, is the water tank for the stock well up and the windmill working?"

"Yep, what would you like?"

"Maybe a couple gallon jugs of water for the bathroom. We'll need it before morning."

25

They sat down to a dinner of cold chicken and mashed potatoes. Jacques spiced it up with a tomato from the garden. When Marie frowned at his use of food that would not spoil quickly, he said "There's a lot more on the vine."

TUESDAY AUGUST 16, NOON

New York, NY. There was a fire overnight in the apartment of Ivan. He was found dead, presumably from smoke inhalation. He was a known smoker, so the police immediately knew the answer to what had happened. If they had checked, they would have found his blood-alcohol level at a point indicating dead drunk. They didn't check, there was too much to do elsewhere. Lipstick stained cigarette butts had been carefully removed from the ash tray last night to simplify their decision.

York counted out the $20,000 dollars left after funding Ivan and $10,000 to have him dissappear. He dressed and went out to deposit the $20 K in his bank. There were no banks open.

Des Plaines, Il. - As his boss had instructed, Jerry turned on the CB handset at 8am and shortly after heard his boss saying that they would try opening the store at noon. Would Jerry please come in about 11:45?. When he had gone, Sue turned on the handset and for a while heard nothing but a low level noise, then:

"Anyone out there? This is trucker Tom and you ain't gonna believe what I tell ya I saw comin' through Chicago. The lights were out and there weren't no signals at the road crossins. You could hear the horns honkin' from a mile away. When I got to a major intersection, there was a cop there with a flashlight tryin' to get traffic movin right. It was hopeless and when there was a small fender bender, he yelled at 'em to give each other their phone number and just go home. Hey, anybody out there?"

The signal went off and the low noise returned. Sue didn't think before she pushed the key.

"Trucker Tom, this is Sue in Des Plaines and where are you headed for."

"Howdy Sue. I'm headed for Iowa, but I ain't got the fuel to get there. Are there any stations pumping in Des Plaines? I tried to get some diesel last night. There was a long line and when I got to the pump he said he was pumpin' on auxiliary power, but he was outta diesel. At least he said he was sorry. Well I'd bought a lot from him over the years. That's the least he could say."

"Hey, Tom. I don't know of anyone pumping diesel, but there are a lot of stations on the main route. Hope you can make it that far."

"Thanks, Sue. Hey anyone ? I need diesel between Chicago and Des Plaines. Anyone?"

NORAD-UNDERGROUND COMMAND CENTER - General North and his aides had been up all night and managed to establish, via one operational satellite, communication with a dozen military bases in the U.S. The bases were advised to close the gates, use backup power only at hospitals and headquarters and stand by for further orders. He picked up the phone reserved for the UCC contact and punched the call button.

"This is Gates, General North. What do you want?"

"I'm calling to tell you we have rudimentary communication with a dozen military bases and to ask what your plans are at this point."

"What do the bases tell you about the state of the electric grid?"

"It varies widely. There are several small towns in the mid-west that have local power and are not connected to the grid. Unfortunately that does not include any cities of sizable population. In the southeast, the Tennesee Valley Authority, TVA hydro generation appears to be operating and parts of the grid are up, probably including a few nuclear plants. However, generally the Eastern Grid is down. There are no lights in New York City. The Texas Grid is down with only a few small locations on local power. In the Western Grid there were lights on in downtown Los Angeles, and on the Central Coast. Otherwise, it was dark. We surveyed all of that by satellite last night."

"Good work, North. We did find the head of FERC and he is here with us. His view is pretty dark. Says we are not likely to be back up completely for at least a week and that it may be longer for New York City. I think he may be overstating it to build his status, but as of now, he's our only expert."

"Does he propose any plans ?"

"Yeah, one that's rather weird. He says we should impose military government at oil storage and refineries in the Texas region and wherever there still is power to keep them refining gas and diesel. Then get fuel trucks in there to load up and drive to refuel filling stations in the areas that have no power. Says they can first load the tanks of the stations and from there the tanks of trucks using hand pumps. The trucks will go out to farms to bring in produce. Sounds strange to me. I'd like to see us print and send out money as fast as we could. That's simpler"

"How would you distribute that money, Gates? Most of the countries wealth is tied up in charge cards and banks. Neither are reachable now. However, his trucker plan does get at the primary problem of food. Does he have any ideas about water?"

"That's part of his strange plan. says fueled trucks can load up water from rivers and take it into town to fill up containers the people bring to a central point. Says police cars with loudspeakers can cruise around announcing where the food and water will be available."

"What do the people from the Pentagon say about that military control of the refineries and storage?"

"They don't have a problem with it. They are gathered around maps, figuring which base will do what. They even suggested control of fuel storage depots in the southeast using the same trucking idea."

"Is POTUS going to OK this."

"He's thinking about it now. You know he has a lot of supporters in the oil industry. This isn't easy. However, we could print money and distribute it to the refineries very easily."

"OK, Gates. What can NORAD do to help now?"

"Keep us up to date on your satellite surveillance. How many do you have?"

"Just two. The CME took out nearly every thing we had up, except for one communication unit and a surveillance unit in synchronous orbit. I don't think there are any commercial satellites operational. Would you give me a call when POTUS decides?"

"OK, thanks for the communication paths. Talk with you later."

WEDNESDAY AUGUST 17 NOON

<u>Des Plaines, Il.</u> - Jerry saw a food truck on this way back from the store and stopped to see what he could buy with the fast disappearing cash in his pocket. Inside the truck was Julio Gomez, dishing out paper plates of food and taking in cash as fast as customers appeared. Jerry went home with four cheese enchiladas and a non-descript bottle of clean looking water. That took a ten dollar bill. It was just about the end of the cash between he and Sue, but the refrigerator was getting empty and what was left looked very suspicious. This would go well.

Julio surveyed his stock of food and his pocket of cash and decided it was time for a trip to the grocery store. His truck passed two grocery stores that were closed before finding one open. He walked in to find only a few customers and shelves that were nearly empty.

In a cart he assembled a case of frijoles refritos and 20 pounds of brown rice plus 200 paper plates. When he got to the checker he heard, "You know it's cash only."

"I know that, but how much cash for this?"

"Lemme see. I guess that about 80 dollars would cover that."

"You crooks are fortunate the cops are too busy to check up on you. How about 60 dollars?"

"Have you got it?"

"Yeah."

"OK, but make it 70."

Julio dug into his pocket without showing what was in there and then added to it to total 70 dollars. Handing it over, he wheeled the cart to the door and emptied it into the back of the truck. Thinking that he would make at least 150 dollars on this and have rice left over, he smiled. After half an hour the truck wheeled to a new residential neighborhood. The side panel went up and he began serving rice and beans on paper plates, just like Abuelita used to do.

The last two of the customers came up to the side of the truck.

"This gun is loaded. My partner is gonna come in your back door with another gun. If you don't do as we say, you're dead."

The following morning the truck was found with the dead body of Julio inside, a single gunshot wound to the back of his head. The truck was parked on a side road. Its fuel tank was siphoned, both the drinking water and the grey water tanks were empty and the propane tank had been unbolted and removed. A cop was alerted by hikers, looking for fruit on nearby trees. He knew how hopeless the case was with limited communication, but he photographed it and called a local minister who had volunteered to pick up bodies and take them to the address on their drivers license. The cop checked the billfold, and as expected found only two dollar bills.

Calgary, "Jacques, I'm worried about our kids who live in town. We're doin OK out here, but they are in a worse spot. Maybe we should try to get them out here with us?"

"I've been worried about that. I didn't know how we could reach them until I remembered in 2013 back in Quebec people discovered that the old round dial phones would work even with the grid down. I've got one on a shelf in the barn, but I don't know about the kids. The older one had a dial phone that he treasured as a relic from the grid failure in Quebec. Maybe he put it on line?"

"Let's get ours and see what we can do."

When it was connected, Jacques picked up the handset and heard a dial tone. With a big smile on his face he dialed the number of his oldest son. The ring was heard for several times, then a voice said, "Etienne here."

"Hello son. We been worried about you folks and thought we'd see how you are."

"Took you a while to remember that old phone. How are you and mama doing?"

"We're in good shape out here, growing our own food you know. We wondered if it was maybe time to move you and the rest of the family from Calgary to here at the farm until this thing gets fixed?"

"That's a great idea. I've still got some gas in my truck, but I talked with Charles and he said he's empty. Let me get all of us together with a few of our things and we'll see you before sundown. Hope mom can fix dinner for four adults and five kids. We are getting a little hungry."

"Sounds great. Your mom says that's the best news she's heard. I'll put up some cots in the barn and the kids will like sleeping on blankets on top of hay. Matbe you could bring extra bed clothes. We'll look to see all of you before dark."

It all worked out and Marie fixed three chickens and a big salad of tomatoes, lettuce and onions. It was like old home week.

Inevitably the talk turned to the situation in the city.

"It has not been too bad. The stores sold all their food and water by Tuesday noon. We were still living off our refrigerator, but reaching the end when you called in. You couldn't have timed it better. Looks like the kids have had a heavy day. Maybe if you could let us have one of those lanterns, we could all get to bed in the barn?"

NORAD-UCC- On Tuesday night the presidents decision to impose military control on refineries and fuel storage depots was implemented. The pentagon officers had previously instructed military bases to stockpile hand pumps capable of handling gasoline or diesel fuel.

Cooperation from truckers was good. The refineries and storage depots were granted excellent prices for the products put into the trucks. Each truck carried as passenger a military officer or non-com who signed the draft order for the produce loaded. The loads were then dispersed at no cost to people who gathered at central locations. Cop cars with loud speakers announced the location of the unloading. The military bases were instructed to transfer meals to eat, Meals Ready to Eat, MREs to all hospitals, truckers and police units with enough included for the cops families.

SUNDAY AUGUST 21 NOON-

Des Plaines, Il. - The refrigerator had long ago been cleaned. Cop cars had come through announcing that food would be available while it lasted at Chattaqua Park and water could be had from the nearby river. Jerry looked worried. "There isn't enough gas to drive to Chattaqua park more than once more. I've got an idea."

"Thank God. I'm all out of ideas."

"Suppose we fix up the station wagon so we can live in it and then drive to the park. We can park it there and sleep overnight, then pick up food each morning. If anybody complains we can say that if they have some gas for us, we will drive home."

"You know, that just might work. We are surely out of everything here. We'll fix up the wagon, lock the house and go!"

They took a mattress from a twin bed and with the seats down in back, placed it on the deck. Some bed clothes, a few water bottles and a couple rolls of toilet paper and they were ready to go.

When they arrived at the park, they saw that a few others had got the same idea, but not many and the cars were far apart. They parked the wagon in the shade of the pine trees just southeast of the swimming pool and collected some water from the pool to last the night. The wagon bed allowed sleep better than they expected. They rose with the sun and waited for the truckers with food. About mid morning people began to walk in from the United Methodist

34

Campground nearby. Soon the truckers arrived and Sue saw that they would be vegetarians whether they liked it or not. But without cash and gas there was little choice and it certainly beat going hungry.

Calgary, Alb. - The chicken coops were nearly exhausted when Marie called a halt on Friday and suggested they slaughter one of the cattle. The three men undertook this chore and in little time had stretched the skin and cut up the meat. They robbed the store of winter firewood and built a bed of coals in the old grate behind the barn that had served many parties in earlier years. By sundown the cow was cooked and a handsome feast set out. The pieces not used immediately were wrapped in plastic bags, tied shut and sunk in the stock tank with rocks. Jacques explained, "It's an old Indian trick we learned in Quebec. The beef will keep quite a while without any air on it and maintained at a decent temperature right after it's been cooked. damned smart those Indians."

The beef made a good lantern lit dinner. Afterward three very tired men went straight to bed.

San Antonio, Tx. - Romi and Julia had celebrated their 65th wedding anniversary with friends on September 7, just 2 weeks ago. Last night they went to bed in their hot, dark condo with a few memories of their lives still intact. Just after dawn today, Romi awakened to find Julia absolutely still, mouth open and not breathing. He tried to start her breathing as he had been taught in safety class. She remained still. Heat and dehydration had done their work. After a few minutes of effort, he collapsed across her chest, his mouth open, but unable to make a sound as he gasped. Later tears rolled from his eyes and he found himself able to make a sound. He rushed to a neighboring condo. After his knock the door opened a crack.

"Julia has died and I can't bring her back. I need help, I don't know what to do."

"Oh my God. I'll get the wife. Stay here and we'll go back with you."

The three returned to Romi's condo and verified that indeed the end had come for Julia. The wife volunteered that she heard yesterday the mortuary would not pick up bodies as they had only enough fuel to drive to the cemetery.

With two other friends they picked a favorite dress, wrapped Julia in the bed sheet, loaded her in the car and drove to the nearest mortuary. The proprieter helped them unload and then said to Romi. "I have to tell you that with no lights or power we cannot do a decent job of embalming. I suggest you pick a casket and we drive to the cemetery this afternoon at three. That will give you time to inform a few friends."

At three about a dozen people gathered where over fifty would normally have been to recognize Julia's volunteer work with Red Cross and in the local school. Romi surveyed this with increased pain.

St. LOUIS, MO- With the lights off, many elderly people were in jeopardy in the early morning hours. Their sense of balance was near zero and in the dark it was easy to fall. One lady fell in her apartment, breaking her lower leg. With her cane she beat on the wall until the neighbors came to investigate the trouble. They could not think how to move her until they found an ironing board in the closet. They carefully rolled it under her and secured the leg with torn dish towels. They had no way to call an ambulance, but did carry the board with it's groaning load out to their station wagon. At the hospital people from the Emergency Room carried her inside. The neighbors trailed along to see that she was well treated. What they saw was controlled chaos with many similar accidents, cots in the hallways and waiting room. The followed the ironing board into the X-Ray room, then back to the waiting room. Two hours later an aide motioned them to follow into the surgery room. A very tired surgeon examined the leg and the X-Ray after she had been moved from the ironing board to the surgery table. "I'm going to have to put in a metal brace and screws. It will be a while." Then to the person nearby, "Do we have anaesthetic for an hour and a half?"

"Just barely."

"Mary, go see if you can find more anesthetic. Now let's start."

Mary did not find more anesthetic and the sweating surgeon hurried for just over an hour.

"All right, that does it. Take her to recovery, wherever that is now."

THE MONEY MARKET

On Monday, August 15, the U.S. financial markets in New York City were frozen. This was known almost immediately in Europe through the Trans Atlantic Cable. Europe also knew of the solar flare from effects in Scandinavia and Iceland. There was some concern in the London, Berlin and Paris markets, but it was late in the day and most everyone waited to see what would happen overnight.

At the Tuesday opening of the market there was some surprise that power was still off in much of the U.S. and particularly in New York City. The dollar began to fall with respect to other world currencies. By mid afternoon the fall accelerated as the power was still off in New York. The dollar fell over 15% and a few brave souls began to buy the Chinese Yuan, which was up 5% at the close.

On Wednesday the dollar dropped another 10% and the Yuan was up 10%. A halt was called in dollar trading and the International Monitary Fund, IMF called an emergency meeting. The IMF determines the international reserve currency which is used in trades between nations. For example, unless a nation-nation currency agreement exists, one nation buying oil or goods from another must convert its money to the reserve currency to pay for those goods.

On Thursday the IMF, noting no improvement in the U.S. power situation, halted use of the dollar as the world reserve currencies and approved the Chinese Yuan for a reserve currency. A proposal by OPEC of a bundle based on Mid-East currencies was put in consideration as an additional reserve currency. It would be called the Opie. Trading in the dollar-denominated bonds was resumed. The value fell 15% in the first day.

SUNDAY AUGUST 28 NOON

Calgary, Alb. - Saturday night they could see a red light and smoke from downtown Calgary. It was clear that a house was on fire and there was no water to put it out. Charles wondered if this was the work of gangs out of food and angry about everything. This set the thinking of the group on what they might do if a gang came up the road from town. The mood darkened as nothing seemed possible. It was evident they had cattle and were a good target.

Etienne rose and with a slight smile said, "There's something we could try. People on the road are visible for maybe 15 minutes before they could get here. Suppose we take Jacques hunting rifle and set up some targets readily visible from the road. We put the kids and ladies in the house. Then the three of us men sit down out there if there is a group coming. When they get within hearing distance we start a shooting contest, taking turns. After each shot we yell and take on about the accuracy or lack thereof. We might even have some beer bottles with yellow liquid in them. After each shot we all take a swig and yell and laugh again. If they are friends we know, they'll yell back and offer to match our shooting. But, I bet if they are out for loot, they'll think twice and likely go back to town."

There was a chance to test the idea on Sunday about lunch time. A group of three young men walked on the road from Calgary. As planned, the ranchers sat down and after several drinks of watered tea began to yell and derate each others marksmanship. This lead to a trial shot and a yell.

"Ten, right in the tigers head!" That lead to more dispute and a trial shot from another rancher.

"Ten, a real ten, right in the squirrels eye."

This went on for a few minutes and the three young men turned and walked back to Calgary.

Dinner that night was some of the beef stored in the stock tank and grilled on the grate behind the barn. Jacques made a salad from the last of the tomatoes and lettuce from the garden.

NORAD-UCC- General North picked up the phone to the UCC. "Let me speak with Gates."

"Good evening general. Our man from FERC has been tying up the phone all day, what's up?"

"We are going to try to bring up the grid tonight. Cop cars with loudspeakers will be out tonight in major residential areas all over the country. Their message will be an appeal to turn off the switches on the air conditioning so we can bring back the grid, i.e. turn it off now so you can use it tomorrow."

"Do you think it will work?"

"About two hours after sunset we'll know. Until then we'll hope. We are using our satellite communication to military bases to coordinate the restart. The bases will talk to military vehicles located at the major stations. The restart will move from east to west, just like the CME did."

"How can POTUS watch this?"

"He can't watch it, but I'll put a senior officer on this phone to describe what we see here from the satellite in synchronous orbit."

"Let us hope!"

THE RETURN OF THE GRID

Just two hours after sunset on the east coast, with the TVA hydro stations already up, fossil fuel and nuclear generating stations synchronized with the TVA and closed their connections to the grid. In most cases these worked the first time, but after 5 minutes all were connected. Then the north portion of the eastern grid with it's controls repaired from the CME burning, began to synchronize and reconnect. Street lights went on along the coast all the way up to Maine.

Chicago closed on line shortly after. Then there was a wait as the western grid began to build. After 30 minutes most of the west was up and synchronization to the Eastern Grid was eased by the HVDC connection in the Dakotas. The Western grid synchronized and connected with the Eastern Grid. This was reported to POTUS in the UCC.

The Texas grid was connected within it's own region, but not yet synchronized with the East and West grids. Slowly synchronization was approached in the Texas panhandle where connection would be made to the western grid. When the moment came connection failed and the circuit breakers refused to reclose. This was tried again 5 minutes later and this time it held. The connection to the Eastern grid was then easy and worked the first time.

NORAD was now able to report to POTUS that the U.S. grid was re-established. Cheers were heard throughout the UCC.

"This is the President. Good work NORAD. When can we leave the UCC and go back to daylight?"

"Good evening Mr. President and congratulations! Within an hour you should be able to see the satellite image of lights on in the U.S. However, I would suggest you delay departure until late tomorrow afternoon to be sure that everything holds with air-conditioning back on."

"All right, then we will schedule a TV announcement for tomorrow morning. I'll be sure to give NORAD good credit."

"Thank you sir. You may wish to give some credit to FERC. They were instrumental in coordinating the re-connection."

"Good idea. Turn on your TV at 10 EST tomorrow."

ACROSS THE PACIFIC

Randy and Francis boarded a plane for the motherland at San Francisco Airport. In the first class section they celebrated their recall, surely for promotion. They were drinking their second vodka martini when the bomb in the luggage compartment exploded. The plane broke apart and dropped from 35,000 feet into one of the deeper parts of the Pacific Ocean. "Grandfather" had ordered funeral flowers for Randy's parents in the motherland and for the San Francisco consulate. His assistant released the orders as instructed, as soon the news was received concerning the loss of the plane.

In New York city, York fell in front of a subway train and died immediately. This time "Grandfather" was surprised, but sent flowers to the NYC consulate with instructions that the body was to be sent back to the motherland.

General North and the FBI searched carefully the records of all stations of the electric grid. They found only that stations shut down as they normally would do when presented with excess load. The explosion and fire in the Manhattan 12th street station looked suspicious, but the fire destroyed everything. The transformer oil ignited and air inflow from the underground cable ducts fed this to an extreme temperature. All possible evidence was reduced to a grimy mound of slag on the broken concrete floor. General North was suspicious, but had to admit there was no evidence to show that the grid collapse was anything but a follow on to the large CME of that Monday.

The remaining heads of station adopted a grim silence and viewed the events as anything but coincidence. One by one they were recalled to the motherland for promotion, but with tickets by ship. None of them fell overboard.

"Grandfather" retired to his home in the forest to enjoy a double scotch on the rocks.

Printed in the United States
By Bookmasters